I0606874

Samuel Freedley

Executor's sale, estate of Dr. Samuel Freedley, deceased

catalogue of rare botanical, medical, and miscellaneous books ... to be sold at

public sale on Monday and Tuesday afternoons, June 11 and 12, 1888, at 2 o'clock

Samuel Freedley

Executor's sale, estate of Dr. Samuel Freedley, deceased
catalogue of rare botanical, medical, and miscellaneous books ... to be sold at
public sale on Monday and Tuesday afternoons, June 11 and 12, 1888, at 2 o'clock

ISBN/EAN: 9783742812827

Manufactured in Europe, USA, Canada, Australia, Japa

Cover: Foto ©Andreas Hilbeck / pixelio.de

Manufactured and distributed by brebook publishing software
(www.brebook.com)

Samuel Freedley

Executor's sale, estate of Dr. Samuel Freedley, deceased

CATALOGUE.

1 Velpeau. Maladies des Yeux, etc. 5 vols. 16mo.
2 Boerhaave, H. Tractatus de Viribus Medicamentorum, etc. 6 vols. 16mo.
3 Tissot, Dr. Advice and Diseases. 3 vols. 16mo., old calf. Edinburgh, 1772.
4 Douglas on the Muscles, etc. 9 vols. 12mo., cloth.
5 Croserio. Obstetrics, Cook's Obstetrics, Record Venereal Diseases. 3 vols. 12mo., cloth.
6 Lobb, T. Dissolvents of the Stone. 12mo., old calf. London, 1739.
7 Griffith & Rees. On the Blood and Urine. 12mo., cloth. Philadelphia, 1848.
8 Baglivi, Geo. Practice of Physick, and on the Tarantula. 2 copies. 12mo., old calf. London.
9 Griffith & Huxham. On Fevers, etc. 7 vols. 12mo., sheep.
10 Boerhaave's Aphorisms. 2 copies. In English and Latin. 12mo. London, 1735.
11 Brera on Verminous Diseases, etc. 7 vols. 12mo., old calf.
12 Astruc, J. Diseases of Women, Clark of Females, etc. 7 vols. 8vo., sheep.
13 Healde. Pharmacopœia, Travernier's Surgery, etc. 10 vols. 8vo., sheep.
14 Bateman. Cutaneous Diseases, Coxe's Medical Dictionary, etc. 10 vols. 8vo., sheep.
15 Philip, J. P. W. On Fevers; also, Lawrence on Ruptures. 3 vols. 8vo., sheep. London.
16 Travers, B. Surgical Essays; also, Abernethy's Surgical Observations. 3 vols. 8vo., sheep. London.
17 Travers, B. Diseases of the Eye; also, Brodie on the Joints. 2 vols. 8vo., sheep. London.

18   Abernethy. Theory of Life, and Bollies' Morbid Anatomy, etc. 3 vols. 8vo., sheep. London.
19   Wilson. Physiology, Parrish on Hernia, etc. 4 vols. 8vo., sheep.
20   Evanson. Diseases of Children, Newton on Thoracic Diseases, etc. 3 vols. 8vo., sheep.
21   Williams on the Respiratory Organs, and Gooch's Midwifery. 2 vols. 8vo., sheep.
22   Cooper, Saml. Dictionary of Practical Surgery. 8vo., sheep. London, 1822.
23   Astruc, John. Venereal Diseases. 2 vols. 8vo., sheep. London, 1737.
24   Rayer. Maladies des Reins. 3 vols. 8vo., half calf. Paris, 1839.
25   Cooper, S. Surgery. 2 vols. 8vo., sheep. 1835.
26   Cullen, G. Synopsis. 2 vols. 8vo., old calf. Edinburgh, 1795.
27   Grant, W. On Fevers. 2 vols. 8vo., sheep.
28   Haller, A. Physiology. 2 vols. 8vo., sheep. London.
29   Hippocratis Opera Genuina Recensuit. 4 vols. 12mo., half leather. Lansannæ, 1784.
30   Chapman, N. Therapeutics. 2 vols. 8vo., sheep. Philadelphia.
31   Chaptal, M. J. Chemistry. 4 vols. 8vo., old calf. London, 1807.
32   Hartmann's Theory of Acute Diseases. 4 vols. 12mo., cloth. New York, 1847.
33   Boyer's Surgery. 2 vols. 8vo., sheep.
34   System of Anatomy and Physiology. Illustrated. 3 vols. 8vo., sheep. Edinburgh, 1795.
35   Baldinger, E. G. Opera. 6 vols. in 3. 12mo., old calf. Gottingæ, 1776. ^
36   Baglivi, G. Opera. 2 vols. 12mo., half leather. Parisüs, 1788.
37   Leake, J. On Women. 2 vols. 8vo., sheep.
38   Swieten, G. Van. The Commentaries upon the Aphorisms of Dr. H. Boerhaave. 14 vols. 8vo., old calf. London, 1759.
39   Boerhaave, Dr. H. Lectures. 6 vols, 8vo., old calf. London, 1746.

40 De Haen Antonii. Ratio Medendi in Nosocomio Practico Vindobonensi. 4 vols. 8vo., sheep. 1761.

41 Hahnemann, Saml. Reine Arzncimittellehre. 6 vols. Half sheep. Dresden, 1830.

42 Haen, A. de Praelectiones in Hermanni Boerhaave. 5 vols. 8vo., half leather. Vienna, 1780.

43 Hoffman, Dr. Medicine. 2 vols. 8vo., sheep. London, 1783.

44 Brooks. Practice of Physic. 2 vols. 8vo., leather.

45 Cullen, W. First Lines. 4 vols. 8vo., sheep.

46 Desault's Surgery. 2 vols. ; also, Paris' Pharmacologia, 2 vols. 4 vols. 8vo., sheep.

47 Rush, Benj. Works of. 5 vols. 8vo , half Morocco. Philadelphia, 1809.

48 Hunter, John. Treatise on the Blood. 2 vols. 8vo., sheep. London.

49 Thomson, Thos. Chemistry. 4 vols. 8vo., old calf, Philadelphia.

50 Morgagni, J. B. Diseases. 2 vols. 8vo., calf. Boston, 1824.

51 Good's Study of Medicine. 5 vols. 8vo., sheep. Boston.

52 Otto. Voyage Medicale. 2 vols. half Morocco. Hamburg.

53 Apparatus Medicaminum. 6 vols. 8vo., old calf. Goettingæ, 1793.

54 Bick's Medical Jurisprudence. 2 vols. 8vo., leather. Philadelphia.

55 Darwin, E. Zoonomia. 3d edition. 4 vols. 8vo., half calf. London, 1801.

56 Eberle, J. Materia Medica ; also, Barton's Cullen. 4 vols. in all. 8vo., sheep.

57 Zimmermann's Experience. 2 vols. 8vo , half leather.

58 Sydenham, Thos. The Works of; also, Cuvier's Anatomy. 4 vols. in all. 8vo., sheep.

59 Dorsey's Surgery ; also, Pott's Surgery. In all 4 vols. 8vo., sheep.

60 Pancoast's Wistar. 2 vols. 8vo., sheep. Philadelphia, 1846.

61 Dunglison, R. Therapeutics. 2 vols. 8vo., sheep. Philadelphia, 1846.

62 Horner, W. E. Special Anatomy. 2 vols. 8vo., sheep. Philadelphia, 1851.

63 Sharpey & Quains. Human Anatomy. 2 vols. 8vo., sheep. Philadelphia, 1849.

64 Gibson, Wm. Practice of Surgery. 2 vols. 8vo., sheep. Philadelphia, 1850.

65 Chapman on Fevers; also, Miller's Surgery. 2 vols. 8vo., sheep. Philadelphia, 1845.

66 Lawrence, W Diseases of the Eye. 8vo., sheep. Philadelphia, 1854.

67 Simons, J. F. Chemistry of Man. 8vo., sheep. Philadelphia, 1846.

68 McClellan's Surgery, Chitty's Jurisprudence, etc. 3 vols. 8vo., sheep.

69 Miller's Surgery; also, Fergusson's Surgery. 2 vols. 8vo., sheep. Philadelphia.

70 Churchill. Infants and Children; also, Ashwell on Diseases of Females. 2 vols. 8vo., sheep. Philadelphia.

71 Coxe's Epitome of Hippocrates. 8vo., sheep. Philadelphia.

72 Carpenter's Physiology. 8vo., sheep. Philadelphia.

73 Wilde on the Ear; also, Prout on the Stomach. 2 vols. 8vo., sheep. Philadelphia.

74 Curling on the Testis; also, Diseases of the Nervous System. 2 vols. 8vo., sheep. Philadelphia.

75 Mayo's Pathology; also, Henle's Pathology. 2 vols. 8vo., sheep. Philadelphia.

76 Duparcque on the Uterus; also, Rigby's Midwifery. 2 vols. 8vo., sheep. Philadelphia.

77 Churchill's Midwifery; also, Diseases of Womem; also, Columbat on Diseases of Women. 3 vols. 8vo., sheep. Philadelphia.

78 Gross, S. D. The Urinary Organs. 8vo., sheep. Philadelphia, 1851.

79 Colles, A. Surgery. Solly on the Brain; also, Churchill on Pueperal Fever. 3 vols. 8vo sheep. Philadelphia.

80 Condie on Diseases of Children; also, Taylor's Jurisprudence. 2 vols. 8vo., sheep. Philadelphia, 1845.

81 Carpenter, W. B. Physiology; also, Stokes on the Heart. 2 vols. 8vo., sheep. Philadelphia.

82 Cooper, Sir Astley. On Hernia, The Testis and The Breast. 3 vols. 8vo., sheep. Philadelphia.

83 Ramsbotham's Process of Parturition. 8vo., sheep. Philadelphia.

84 Gross, S. D. Pathological Anatomy. 8vo., sheep. Philadelphia.

85 Morton, S. G. Human Anatomy. 8vo., sheep. Philadelphia.

86 Bichat, X. General Anatomy, 3 vols. 8vo., boards. Boston.

87 Thomas, Sydenham. Opera Medica. 2 vols. 4to., old calf. Genevæ, 1716.

88 De Sauvages, F. B. Nosologia Methodica. 2 vols. 4to., old calf. Amstelodami, 1768.

89 Haller, Alberti V Opera Minora. 3 vols. 4to., old calf. Lansannæ, 1712.

90 Ditto. Vols. 1 and 3 only.

91 Morgagni, J. B. Morborum. 3 vols. 4to., old calf. 1779.

92 Morgagni, John B. Seats and Causes of Disease. 3 vols. 4to., old calf. London, 1669.

93 Haller, A. Von. Bibliotheca Medicinæ Practicæ. 4 vols. 4to., boards. Bernæ, 1776.

94 Parr, B. Medical Dictionary. 2 vols. 4to., old calf. Philadelphia, 1819.

95 Van Helmont, J. B. Oriatrike, or Physick Refined. Scarce. 2 vols. Folio, half board. London, 1662.

96 Henderico, Benj. Græcum Lexicon. 4to., old calf. London, 1816.

97 Quain & Wilson. Anotomical Plates. 2d edition. 4to., cloth. Philadelphia, 1843.

98 Pancoast, Jos. Operative Surgery. 80 Plates. 4to., cloth. Philadelphia, 1844.

99 Ricord, Ph. Illustrations of Syphilitic Disease. 4to., cloth. Philadelphia, 1851.

100 Moreau, F. J. Treatise on Midwifery. 4to., cloth. Philadelphia, 1844.

101 Rayer, P. Diseases of the Skin. 4to., cloth. Philadelphia, 1845.

102 Gluge, Dr. Gottlieb. Atlas der Pathologischen Ana-
      tomic. 2 vols. Folio, full Morocco, gilt. Jena,
      1850.
103 Cl Galeni Pergameni Asiani, Excellentissimi semper,
      post vinicum Hippocratem. 8 vols. in 4. Folio,
      pigskin, clasps. Basileæ, 1569.
104 Motherly, G. Medical Dictionary Folio, sheep.
      London, 1785.
105 Galeni Opera. 8 vols. Folio, red calf. Venetiis, 1576.
106 Caroli Clvsii Atrebatis. Exoticorum Libri Decem.
      Folio, old calf. 1605.
107 Forbes, Edw. Monograph of the British Naked Eye
      Medusæ. Colored plates. Folio, boards. London,
      1848.
108 Diemerbroeck, I. de. The Anatomy of Human Bodies.
      Translated by Wm. Salmon. Curious copperplates.
      Folio, old calf. London, 1694.
109 Hunter, W. Essay on the Diseases Incident to Indian
      Seamen, or Lascars. Folio, boards. Calcutta,
      1804.
110 Description of the Genus Cinchona, etc. 4to., boards.
      London, 1797.
111 Dillenius, John Jac. Historia Muscorum. History of
      Land and Water Mosses and Corals. Illustrated.
      Folio, old calf. London, 1768.
112 Lamarck's Conchology, Illustrated Introduction to.
      Folio, boards. London, 1827.
113 Drury, D. Illustrations of National History. 240
      Colored Figures of Exotic Insects, 4to., boards.
      London, 1770.
114 Guthrie on the Brain. 4to., boards. London, 1842.
115 Bell, John. Engravings of Bones, Muscles and Joints.
      2 vols. 4to., half bound. Philadelphia, 1816.
116 Small Portfolio, containing plates relating to the
      Brain. No title.
117 The Ligaments of the Human Body. 30 plates and
      letterpress. 8vo., boards. London.
118 Farre, J. R. Morbid Anatomy of the Liver. Colored
      illustrations. Folio, boards. London, 1812.
119 Methodus Studii Medici, ab Alberto Haller. 2 vols.
      4to., old calf. Amsterdam, 1751.

120 Swedenborgii, E, Regnum Animale. 4to., old calf.
     Hagæ, 1744.
121 Garnett, Thos. Zoonomia, 46. Half bound. London,
     1804.
122 Scarpa, Antonio. Nervorum Gangliis et Plexubus,
     4to., boards. 1792.
123 Bell, Chas. The Nervous System. 4to., cloth. London,
     1830.
124 Cullen, Wm. Meteria Medica. 2 vols. 4to., old calf.
     Edinburgh, 1789.
125 Gibson, J. M. Diseases of the Eye. Illustrated. 4to.,
     boards. Baltimore, 1832.
126 Heister, L. Medical and Anatomical Cases and Obser-
     vations. 4to., half boards. London, 1755.
127 Douglas, G. Structure of the Human Body. Vol. 1
     only. 4to., old calf. London, 1733.
128 Epps, Geo. N. Spinal Curvature. 4to., cloth. London,
     1849.
129 Baglivi, Georgii. Opera Omnia. 4to., half boards.
     Lugduni, 1704.
130 De Diemerbroeck. Opera Omnia. Anatomica et
     Medica. Portrait. 8vo., half boards. Genevæ, 1687.
131 Pitcarnii, A. Scoto. Britanni Elementa Medicinæ.
     4to., half boards. Hagæ, 1718.
132 Hoffmanni, F. Consultationum et Responsorum Medi-
     cinalium. 4to., half boards. 1734.
133 Bianchi, J. B. Historia Hepatica. 3 vols in 1. 4to.,
     old calf. Genevæ, 1725.
134 Hammond's Hygiene. Military Essays. Physiological
     Memoirs. 3 vols. Unbound. Philadelphia.
135 Thompson, T. Annals of Influenza. 2 copies. 8vo.,
     cloth. London.
136 Churchill on Puerperal Fever; also, Stevens on Asiatic
     Cholera. 2 vols. 8vo., cloth.
137 Bastock, G. Physiology. 8vo., cloth. London.
138 Cooper, Saml. Dictionary. 8vo., sheep. New York.
139 La Roche, R. Yellow Fever. 2 vols. 8vo., cloth.
     Philadelphia, 1855.
140 Gross, Saml. System of Surgery. 2 vols. 8vo., sheep.
     Philadelphia, 1864.
141 Hoffmanni, Friderici. Consultationum et Responsorum
     Medicinalium. 4to., vellum. Halæ Magdebvrcicæ,
     1734.

142   Breynius, Johannes P.   Dissertatio Botanico-Medica
       de Radice Gin-Sem fen Nisi.   With plate.   4to.,
       vellum.   Lugduni, Batavorum, 1700.
143   Roederer, Joannis Georgii.   Oratio de Artis Obstetriciæ
       Præstantia.   4to, vellum.   Gœttingæ, 1752.
144   Breynius, Johannes P.   Fungis Officinalibus et corum
       usu in Medicina.   4to., vellum.   Lugduni, Bata-
       vorum, 1702.
145   Nannoni, D'Angelo.   Trattato Chirurgico delle Malattie
       delle Mammelle.   4to., vellum.   Firenze, 1746.
146   Vespa, Giuseppe.   Dell Arte Obtetricia Trattato.   4to.,
       vellum.   Firenze, 1761.
147   Alberti D. Michæle.   Dissertatio Manguralis Medica,
  ,   de Squilla.   4to., vellum.   Halæ Magdeborgicæ,
       1722.
148   Sennerus, Joannes C.   De Senna.   4to., vellum.   1733.
149   Forster, Guilielmus E.   Aristolochiam.   4to., vellum.
       1719.
150   Harvejus, Guilielmus.   Exercitatio Anatomica de Motu
       Cordis, etc.   4to., vellum.   No title page.
151   Langii, Joh. Mich.   De Herba Borith.   4to., vellum.
       1705.
152   Schulze, Jo. Henr.   De Alœ.   4to., vellum.   Altorfii
       Norimbergensium.
153   Dolfusius, Joh. G.   Cerasologia Medica.   4to., vellum.
       Basileæ, 1717.
154   Clericus, Antonius.   A De Asparago.   4to., vellum.
       Altorfi, 1715.
155   Vatero, Abrahamo.   Ductus Salivalis in Linqua.   4to.,
       vellum.   Wittenbergæ, 1723.
156   Langius, G. J.   Millefolium.   4to., vellum.   1714.
157   Corvinus, G. L.   De Scilla.   4to., vellum.   1715.
158   Wedelii, G. W.   De Centaurio Minori.   4to., vellum.
       1713.
159   Klein, J. C.   De Junipero.   4to., vellum.   1719.
160   Hoffmanni, D. F.   De Balsamo Peruviano.   4to.,
       vellum.   Halæ, 1503.
161   Scheffler, J. C.   De Asaro.   4to., vellum.   1721.
162   Scheferus, J. D.   De Chamomilla.   4to., vellum.   Argen
       to rati, 1700.
163   Bleck, Joannes.   De Betonica.   4to., vellum.   1716.
164   Arragoni, R.   Del Fascino.   4to., vellum.   Verona.

165 Wedellio, G. W. De Terebinthina. 4to., vellum. Ienæ, 1700.
166 Wedellio, M. J. A. De Camphora. 4to., vellum. Ienæ, 1697.
167 Houck, F. De Hyperico. 4to., vellum. Ienæ, 1716.
168 Seiffart. Nitrum. 4to., vellum. 1716.
169 Franco, G. Malum Citreum. 4to., vellum. Heidelbergæ, 1686.
170 Petzschius, Chris. H. De Millefolio Germ. 4to., vellum. Halæ Magdeburgical, 1719.
171 Friderici, Johannis A. De Aloe. 4to., vellum. Ienæ, 1670.
172 Kirchmariero, M. C. De Coralio Balsamo et Saccharo. 4to., vellum. 1661.
173 Albino, Bernhardo. De Tabaco. 4to., vellum. Trancofurti.
174 Wedellio, G. De Cuscuta. 4to., vellum. 1715.
175 Faschio, A. H. De Castoreo. 4to., vellum. 1677.
176 Coleri, Johannis. De Bombyce. 4to., vellum. 1665.
177 Trommann, J. C. De Castore vel Fibro von Biber. 4to., vellum. 1686.
178 Albini, B. De Cantharidibus. 4to., vellum. 1687.
179 Heinsio, M. U. De Alce. 4to., vellum. 1681.
180 Rolfinck et Albino. De Cervo. 4to., vellum. Berolin, 1686.
181 Schrœckins, Lucas. De Moscho. 4to., vellum. 1667.
182 Bianchi, V. Parere. 4to., vellum. Venete, 1620.
183 Auctore de Ambra et Succino. 4to., vellum, 1698.
184 Burrows, G. M. Treatise on Insanity. 8vo., one half, Morocco. London, 1828.
185 Ellis, Sir W. C. Treatise on Insanity. 8vo., half Morocco. London, 1838.
186 Galt, John M. Treatise on Insanity. 8vo., half Morocco. New York, 1846.
187 Ray, I. Treatise on the Medical Jurisprudence of Insanity. 8vo., half Morocco. Boston, 1838.
188 Velpeau, A. A. L. M. Midwifery. 8vo., half Morocco. Philadelphia, 1845.
189 Ley, H. On Croup; also, Philip on Health. 2 vols. 8vo., cloth. London, 1830–36.
190 Johnson, Geo. Diseases of the Kidneys. 8vo., cloth. London, 1852.

191 Prichard on Insanity, Malgaigne's Operative Surgery, etc. 3 vols. 8vo., sheep.
192 Pott, Percivall. On the Hydrocele. 2 vols. 8vo., sheep. London, 1767.
193 Crickton, A. On Mental Derangement. 2 vols. 8vo., half calf. London, 1798.
194 Dewee's Practice, On Children, System of Midwifery. 3 vols. 8vo., sheep.
195 Wilson, P. W. Febrile Diseases. 2 vols. 8vo., sheep. Hartford, 1816.
196 Parry, C. H. Medical Writings. 2 vols. 8vo., boards. London.
197 Christison, Robt. Poisons. Benedict's Compendium, Harrison's Anatomy, and Galt's Practice. 4 vols. 8vo., sheep.
198 Lavosier's Chemistry, Hosack's Practice, Edinburgh Dispensatory, and Armstrong on Fevers. 4 vols. 8vo., sheep.
199 Hewson on Syphilis, Cullen's Practice, etc. 4 vols. 8vo., sheep.
200 Zimmerman on Dysentery, Parrish's Surgical Observations, etc. 5 vols. 8vo., sheep.
201 Good, J. M. Nosology. 8vo., half calf. London, 1817.
202 Muller's Physiology, Bell on Venereal, etc. 3 vols. 8vo., half sheep.
203 Colles' on Venereal, Richerand's Physiology, Chisholm on Fevers and Physiological Researches. 4 vols.
204 Baunpsfield, on the Spine, Cutbush's Observations, Ayre on Marasmus, Indigeston, Intestines, etc. 6 vols.
205 Elliot's Elements, Rush on the Mind, Hunter on the Mind, Hunter on Venereal, Green on the Skin, Treatise on Physiology, Boisseau on Fevers, Eberle on Children, Gooch on Diseases. 8 vols.
206 Scarpa on Aneurism, Blane on Seamen, Diseases of Females, Hasack's Nosology, Orfila's Chemistry, Beasley on the Mind, Rush on the Voice. 7 vols.
207 American Dispensatory, Hooper's Dictionary, Bertin on the Heart, Brown's Medicine, Moseley's Diseases, and Lieutaud's Synopsis. 6 vols.
208 Laennec on the Chest, Stoke's Lectures, Hall on the Blood, and Louisville Review. 4 vols.

209 Henry's Chemistry, Gross on Bones, Desault's Treatise, Haller's Arteries, and Armstrong on Fevers. 5 vols.
210 Fellowes, Sir Jas. Pestilential Disorder of Andalusia. 8vo., half calf. London, 1815.
211 Clark's Consumption, MacCulloch on Malaria, Rush's Hillary, Paris on Diet, Gamage on Fever, Philips' Inquiry. 6 vols.
212 Aetiology and Semeiology, Pulmonary Consumption, Blackall on Dropsies. 3 vols.
212a Cheyne, Geo. An Essay on Health and Long Life. 8vo., calf. London, 1734.
213 Mead, Richard. Medical Precepts and Cautions. 8vo., sheep. London, 1751.
214 Chisholm on Fever, Mason on Agues, Darry's Treatise, Bell on Wounds, and Darvin's Phytologia. 5 vols.
215 Thomson's Lectures on Inflammations. 8vo., cloth. Philadelphia, 1831.
216 Oesterlere, F. Medical Logic. 8vo., cloth. London, 1855.
217 Jameson, H. G. Epidemic Cholera. 8vo., cloth. Philadelphia, 1855.
218 Channing, W. Etherization in Childbirth. 8vo., cloth. Boston, 1848.
219 Hahnemann, Saml. The Lesser Writings of. 8vo., half roan. New York, 1852.
220 Boismont, A. Buirre De. Hallucinations. 8vo., cloth. Philadelphia, 1853.
221 La Roche on Pneumonia and Malaria, Bronchitis and Pneumonia. 2 vols. 8vo., cloth.
222 Cuvier, Baron. The Mollusca and Radiata, with additions by Edward Griffith and Edward Pidgeon. 8vo., paper. London, 1834.
223 Louis on Yellow Fever, Liston's Practical Surgery, Cooper's Surgery, and Evans on the Endemic Fevers. 4 vols. 8vo., cloth.
224 Hastings on Inflammations, Cure of Hernia, Fashionable Diseases, Aithhorn on Liver Complaints, Coulson on the Hip Joints, Combe's Phrenology, and Abercrombie on Diseases of the Stomach. 7 vols.
225 Smith, S., on Fever. 8vo., cloth. London, 1830.
226 Coley on Infants and Children, Aetiology and Semeiology, Dick on Digestion and Aran on the Heart. 4 vols. 8vo., paper.

227 Hope, J. Diseases of the Heart, Bier's Inquiry, Wilson
     on West Indian Fever, and Paris on Diet. 8vo.,
     boards.

228 Fordyce on Fever, Martyn's Botany, Rush's Lectures,
     Zimmerman on Pride, Cheselden's Anatomy, System
     of Surgery. 6 vols. 8vo., sheep.

229 Lincoln's Botany, Dunn's Euclid, Grant on Fevers,
     Larrey on Wounds, Rush's Essays, Macbride's
     Essay. 6 vols. 8vo., sheep.

230 Mead on the Plague, Mead de Variol et Morbus,
     Beddoes on Consumption, Lectures on Health,
     Hey's Surgery, Astrues on Fevers. 6 vols.

231 History of Health, Power of Medicines, Diseases of
     America, Barry on Consumption, Flora Americæ
     Septentrionalis, Huxham on Fevers, Potts on
     Hydrocele. 7 vols. 8vo., sheep and calf.

232 Lobb, L., on the Smallpox. 8vo., calf. London, 1757.

233 Underwood on Diseases of Children, Chisholm on
     Fever, Monro's Diseases. 3 vols. 8vo., sheep and
     calf.

234 Amman, Jo. Conradus. Cæliu Aureliani, Siccensis,
     Medici Vestusti, Secta Methodici De Morbis Acutis
     and Chronicis. 8vo., full calf. Amstelædami, 1722.

235 Gallois's Experiments, Senae on Fevers, Chisholm on
     Yellow Fever, Alibert on Intermittents, and Rum-
     ford's Essays. 5 vols. 8vo., sheep.

236 Godman's Addresses, Louis' Phthisis, Cooper on Sper-
     matic Cord, Jahr's Pharmacopœia, and Bell's Sur-
     gery. 5 vols. 8vo., sheep and boards.

237 Ash, John. Dictionary of the English Language. 2
     vols. in 1. 8vo., roan. London, 1775. Title page
     partly destroyed.

238 Simon's Pathology, Curie's Homœopathy, Bourgery's
     Surgery, Clark on Fever, Bird on Urinary Deposits,
     Diseases of Females, Mütter on Club Foot, and
     Diseases of the Lungs. 8 vols. Cloth, sheep and
     half Morocco.

239 Jahr, G. H. G. Forty Years' Practice, Burrows on
     Cerebral Circulation, Green on Polypi of the
     Larynx, Lycock on Hysteria, Prickert on Head-
     aches, Blundell on Diseases of Women. Ananthe-
     sia in Surgery, Parker on Syphilitic Diseases. 10
     vols.

240   9 Medical Books, assorted.
241   10   do   do   do
242   Jahr's Homœpathische   Heilmittel   and   Quincy's
        Medical Lexicon.   2 vols.   8vo., half Morocco and
        half calf.
243   8 Medical Books, assorted.
244   10   do   do   do
245   11   do   do   do
246   10   do   do   do
247   8   do   do   do
248   9   do   do   do
249   3   do   do   do
250   Matthæi, C. C.   Preisschrist über das Gilbe Fieber.
        2 vols.   8vo., roan.   Binding defective.
251   Prosperi Alpini de Præsagorida.   8vo., boards.   Lug-
        duni Batavorum, 1701.
252   4 Medical Books, assorted.   Vols. 2 and 3 only.
253   Oeuvies D'Hippocrate.   2 vols.   8vo., paper.   Paris,
        1840 and 1841.
254   6 Medical Books, assorted.
255   5   do   do   do
256   7   do   do   do
257   Johnson on Tropical Climates.   2 vols.   12mo., boards.
258   6 Books, assorted.
259   5   do   do
260   6   do   do
261   3   do   do
262   Marquaidi's Practica Medicinalis; also, Boerhaave's
        Materia Medica.   2 vols.   16mo., vellum and boards.
263   Sterne, Laurence, The Works of.   8 vols. in 4.
        18mo., full calf.   Berwick, 1800.
264   Manuel du Voyageur, Scripture Lessons, and The Royal
        Assassins.   3 vols.   18mo., half calf and cloth.
265   Cowper, Wm.   Poems by.   2 vols.   18mo., sheep.
        London, 1802.
266   More, Hannah.   The Works of.   9 vols.   16mo.,
        sheep.   Philadelphia, 1813.
267   Dolby's British Theatre.   Vols. 1, 2, 3 and 5.   4
        vols. only.   16mo., half calf.   London.
268   American Theatre, containing Tragedies, Comedies and
        Dramas, with alterations by C. Cibber, David Gar-
        rick and others.   Vols. 2, 3 and 4.   4 vols. only.
        16mo., calf.   New York, 1805-6.

269   Bell's British Theatre. Vols. 1, 2, 5, 6, 7, 8, 11, 14, 15,
16, 17, 18, 20 and 21. 14 vols. 16mo., sheep.
London, 1791-2.

270   Chalmus, Alexander. The British Essayists, with
Prefaces Historical and Biographical and Portraits,
with Index. 45 vols. 16mo., full calf. London,
1808.

271   Kotzebue, Augustus Von. His Exile into Siberia.
3 vols. Travels from Berlin to Paris. 3 vols., and
Travels through Italy. 4 vols. 10 vols. in all.
16mo., sheep. London, 1806.

272   Evans, Jno. Shakespeare's Seven Ages. 16mo., half
sheep. London, 1831.

273   Watson on the Bible, Songs of Summer, Zimmerman's
Aphorisms, and vol. 2 of Gay's Poems. 4 vols.
8vo., calf.

274   Shakespeare, Wm. Poems by. 16mo., full calf.
London.

275   Tasso, Torquato. Jerusalem Delivered. 16mo., full
Morocco. New York, 1853.

276   Rotteck, Dr. Karl. Allgemeime Weltgeschichte fur
alle stände. 5 vols. 16mo., half Morocco. Stutt-
gart, 1846.

277   Trenck, Baron Frederic. The Life of. Vols. 1 and 3
only. 2 vols. 16mo., sheep. London, 1788.

278   Moore, George. The Use of the Body in Relation to
the Mind. 16mo., half calf. New York, 1847.

279   Chewell, W. Elements of Morality. 2 vols. 16mo.,
half calf. New York, 1845.

280   Sterm, C. Reflections. 3 vols. 16mo., full calf.
London, 1823-4.

281   Stories from the Classics, Things of the Sea Coast, The
Club, by Puckle. 3 vols. 16mo., cloth.

282   Songs and Ballads of the American Revolution. 12mo.,
cloth. New York, 1856.

283   Tuckerman's Poems; also, Holland's Van Buren. 2
vols. 12mo., cloth and sheep.

284   British Poets. Beattie, Churchill, Collins, Dryden,
Falconer, Goldsmith, Howard, and Wyatt. 14 vols.
12mo., half calf. Boston, 1854.

285   Lesage. Gil Blas. 12mo., half Morocco. Paris, 1848.

286 Richardson, Samuel. Clarissa, or the History of a
     Young Lady. Vols. 5 and 6 only. 2 vols. 12mo.,
     full calf. London, 1774.
287 Richardson, Samuel. History of Sir Charles Grandi-
     son, in a series of letters. Vol. 3 wanting. 6 vols.
     only. 12mo., full calf. London, 1770.
288 Prior, Matthew. Poetical Works of. 2 vols. 12mo.,
     full calf. London, 1779.
289 Collier, Rev. W. Poems on Various Occasions. 2
     vols. 12mo., full calf. London, 1800.
290 Pope. The Beauties of. 2 vols. 16mo., sheep.
     London, 1796.
291 Farrar, C. C. S. The War, Foundation of Faith,
     Foreign Reminiscences, and the Courtship of Miles
     Standish. 4 vols. 12mo., roan, calf, Morocco and
     cloth.
292 Gall, F. J. Treatise on Phrenology. 6 vols. 12mo.,
     cloth. Boston, 1835.
293 Smedley, Rev. E. Reformed Religion in France. 3
     vols. 16mo., half calf. London, 1832.
294 Hemans, Mrs. Complete Works. 2 vols. 16mo.,
     cloth. New York, 1856.
295 Tennyson, In Memoriam. 16mo., half calf. Boston,
     1856.
296 Smith, Adam. The Whole Works of. 5 vols. 16mo.,
     full calf. London, 1822.
297 Schoolcraft, H. R. Algic Researches, comprising
     Inquiries Respecting the Mental Characteristics of
     the North American Indians. Vol. 1 only. 12mo.,
     half calf. New York, 1839.
298 Voltaire, M. de. The Henriade, with the Battle of
     Fontenoy. 12mo., half calf. New York, 1859.
299 Collection of Poems. Vol. 1 wanting. 3 vols. only.
     12mo., full calf. London, 1783.
300 Dick, T. Works of. 4 vols. 12mo., half Morocco.
     Philadelphia, 1835.
301 Pratt, Mr. Miscellanies. 4 vols. 12mo., full calf.
     London, 1785.
302 Tennyson, Alfred. Poems by. 2 vols. 12mo., half
     calf. Boston, 1852.
303 Cumming, Dr. Works of. 4 vols. 12mo., cloth.
     London and New York.

304   Scott, Sir Walter.   Miscellaneous Prose Works of.   6
       vols. 12mo., half calf. Boston, 1829.
305   Parsons, T. W. Poems by. 12mo., half Morocco.
       Boston, 1854.
306   Conrod, Robert T. Poems by. 2 vols. 12mo., half
       calf. Philadelphia, 1852.
307   Boker, Geo. H. Plays and Poems by. Vol. 2 only.
       12mo., half Morocco. Boston, 1856.
308   Tuckerman, H. T. Poems by. 12mo., half Morocco.
       Boston, 1851.
309   Stoddard, R. H. Poems by. 12mo., half calf. Boston,
       1832.
310   Montgomery, Robert. Luther 16mo., half Morocco.
       London, 1842.
311   La Fontaine. Fables of. Illustrated by J. J. Grand-
       ville. 2 vols. 12mo., half calf. New York, 1860.
312   Headley, J. T. The Second War with England. 2
       vols. Old Guard of Napoleon, Adriondack, Ram-
       bles and Sketches, Scott and Jackson, Sacred
       Mountain, Letters from Italy, and Miscellanies and
       Essays. 9 vols. 12mo., half calf. New York,
       1848–56.
313   Walsh's Sketches; also, Analogy of Religion. 2 vols.
       12mo., half Morocco and half calf.
314   Lang, J. D. New South Wales. 2 vols. 12mo., half
       calf. London, 1834.
315   Mackay, Charles. Memoirs of Extraordinary Popular
       Delusions, and the Madness of Crowds. 2 vols.
       12mo., cloth. London, 1856.
316   Sutherland, Peter C. Journal of a Voyage in Baffin's
       Bay and Barrow Straits, in the years 1850–1851,
       with Maps, Plates, and Wood Engravings. 2 vols.
       8vo., cloth. London, 1852.
317   Pynchon, Thos. Ruggles. The Chemical Forces—Heat,
       Light, Electricity. 8vo., cloth. Hartford, 1870.
318   Æschylus. The Tragedies of. Literally Translated,
       with Critical and Illustrative Notes, by Theodore
       A. Buckley; also, The Iliad of Homer. Literally
       Translated, with Explanatory Notes, by Buckley
       8vo., half calf. New York, 1856.
319   The Book and its Story. 8vo., half calf. Philadelphia,
       1855.

320 Johnson, Samuel. Lives of the Most Eminent English
Poets. 2 vols. 8vo., half calf. New York, 1861.
321 Hunt, Leigh. Works of. 4 vols. 8vo., half calf.
New York, 1857.
322 Addison, Joseph. The Works of. 6 vols. 8vo., half
calf. New York, 1857.
323 Pascal, Blaise. The Provincial Letters of. 8vo., half
calf. New York, 1861.
324 Moses, Hannah. Works of. 2 vols. 8vo., half calf.
New York, 1857.
325 Hood, Thomas. Complete Poetical Works of. 2 vols.
8vo., half calf. Boston, 1856.
326 Smollett, Thomas. Miscellaneous Works of, with a
Memoir of the Author by Thomas Roscoe. 6 vols.
8vo., half calf. New York, 1860.
327 Fielding, Thomas. The Miscellaneous Works of, containing Tom Jones, Amelia, Jos. Andrews and Jona-
than Wild. 4 vols. 8vo., half calf. New York,
1857.
328 Irving, Washington. The Works of. 15 vols. 8vo.,
full calf. New York, 1851.
329 Elliott, Hon. Wm. Carolina Sports by Land and
Water. 12mo., cloth. New York, 1859.
330 Bury, Baroness Blaze de. Memoirs of the Princess
Palatine. 8vo., cloth. London, 1853.
331 Carysfort, John J. Dramatic and Narrative Poems by.
2 vols. 8vo., half calf. London, 1810.
332 Byron, Lord. The Works of. Illustrated. 4 vols.
8vo., full calf. Boston, 1854.
333 Howitt, Cook and Soudon, Kirke White and Words-
worth. Poetical Works of. 3 vols. 8vo., cloth.
Boston.
334 Ellet, E. F. The Women of the American Revolution.
Vol. 1 only. Also, Life of General Putnam. 2 vols.
12mo., cloth.
335 Rossetti, Maria F. A Shadow of Dante. 12mo., cloth.
Boston, 1872.
336 Caroli a Linné. Genera Plantarum. 12mo., half calf.
Francofinti, 1789.
337 Fries, Elias. Systema Mycologicum sistens Fungorum.
2 vols. 12mo., full calf. Gryphiswaldial, 1821.
338 Baldwin, S. D. Armageadon. 8vo., cloth. Cincinnati.

339   Hughes, T. M.   An Overland Journey to Lisbon.   2 vols.   8vo., cloth.   London, 1847.

340   Bolingbroke, Viscount.   The Philosophical Works of. 5 vols.   8vo., full calf.   London, 1754.

341   Bolingbroke, Viscount.   The Works of.   8 vols.   8vo., half calf.   London, 1809.

342   History of Paris.   3 vols.   8vo., half roan.   London, 1825.

343   Elton, C. A.   Specimens of the Greek and Roman Classic Poets.   3 vols.   8vo., half calf.   Philadelphia, 1854.

344   Franklin, Benjamin.   Memoirs of the Life and Writings of.   Written by himself.   6 vols.   8vo., sheep. Philadelphia, 1818.   Water stained.

345   Johnson, Samuel.   The Works of.   6 vols.   8vo., full calf.   London, 1825.

346   Montagu, Lady Mary Wortley.   Letters and Works of.   2 vols.   8vo., half Morocco.   Paris, 1837.

347   Denon, Vivant.   Travels in Upper and Lower Egypt. 3 vols.   8vo., half roan.   London, 1803.

348   Reid, Thomas.   The Works of.   3 vols.   8vo., full calf.   New York, 1822.

349   Rollin, Chas.   Ancient History.   4 vols.   8vo., sheep. New York, 1825.   Binding defective and water stained.

350   Shakespeare, W.   The Works of.   With Readings, Notes, a Life of the Poet, and a History of the Early English Stage, by J. Payne Collier.   9 vols. 8vo., full calf.   London, 1844.

351   Gibbon, Edward.   History of the Roman Empire. Vol. 8 wanting.   11 vols.   8vo., sheep.   London, 1818.   Binding defective.

352   Cobbett, Wm.   Porcupine's Works.   Exhibiting a Faithful Picture of the United States of America. 12 vols.   8vo., sheep.   London, 1801.

353   Blair, Hugh.   Lectures on Rhetoric and Belles Letters. 2 vols.   8vo., sheep.   Dublin, 1789.

354   Robertson, W.   History of the Reign of the Emperor Charles V.   2 vols.   8vo., half calf.   London, 1809.   Water stained.

355   Barriere, Mm.   Berville et.   Memoires du Baron de Besenval.   2 vols.   8vo., half calf.   Paris, 1821.

356 Home's Sketches of the History of Man. 4 vols. 8vo.,
sheep. Edinburgh, 1788.

357 Wraxall, N. W. Memoirs of the Courts of Berlin,
Dresden, Warsaw and Vienna. 2 vols. 8vo., calf.
London, 1806.

358 George the Third, his Court and Family. 2 vols. 8vo.,
half calf. London, 1824.

359 Diary Illustrative of the Times of George the Fourth
4 vols. 8vo., half calf. London, 1838.

360 Thomson, Mrs. A. T. Memoirs of the Court of Henry.
the Eighth. 2 vols. 8vo., half calf. London, 1826.

361 Private Memoirs of the Court of Louis XVIII. 2 vols.
8vo., half calf. London, 1830.

362 Walsh, Rev. R. Notices of Brazil in 1828 and 1829.
2 vols. 8vo., half calf. London, 1830.

363 Hallam, H. Constitutional History of England. 3
vols. 8vo., half calf. London, 1854.

364 Bissett, R. History of the Reign of George III. 3
vols. 8vo., half calf. Philadelphia, 1828.

365 Wraxall, N. Memoirs of the Kings of France, of the
Race of Valois. 2 vols. in 1. 8vo., half calf.
London, 1777.

366 Hume, Smollett & Bissett. History of England.
Bound separately. 9 vols. 8vo., sheep. Philadelphia, 1821.

367 Ainsworth, Wm. Harrison. Saint James; also Guy
Fawkes.

368 Ainsworth's Dictionary. 8vo., sheep. Philadelphia,
1812.

369 Koster, H. Travels in Brazil. 2 vols. 8vo., half calf.
London, 1817.

370 Sanderson, John. Biography of the Signers to the
Declaration of Independence. 9 vols. 8vo., half
Morocco. Philadelphia, 1820.

371 Bennett, George. Wanderings in New South Wales.
2 vols. 8vo., half calf. London, 1834.

372 Lay, G. T. The Chinese as they Are. 8vo., half calf.
London, 1841.

373 Goldsmith, O. The Miscellaneous Works of. 4 vols.
8vo., half calf. London, 1821.

374 Lal Mohan. Life of the Amir Dost Mohammed Khan,
of Kabul. 2 vols. 8vo., half calf. London, 1846.

375 Robertson, W. History of America. 3 vols. 8vo.,
     half calf. London, 1821.
376 Baillie, Joanna. Dramas by. 3 vols. 8vo., full calf.
     London, 1836.
377 Baillie, Joanna. Metrical Legends of Exalted Charac-
     ters. 8vo., full calf. London, 1821.
378 Baillie, Joanna. Series of Plays. 3 vols. 8vo., full
     calf. London, 1806.
379 Goldsmith, O. Poetical Works of. 8vo., full Morocco.
     London, 1845.
380 Memorandums of a Residence in France. 8vo., half
     calf. London, 1816.
381 Hallam, H. View of the State of Europe. 2 vols.
     8vo., half calf. London, 1841.
382 Odeleben, Baron Von. Campaign in Saxony in the
     Year 1813. 2 vols. 8vo., half calf. London, 1820.
383 Chandler, Richard. Travels in Asia Minor and Greece.
     2 vols. 8vo., half calf. Oxford, 1825.
384 Laborde, Alexander de. A View of Spain. With
     plates. 6 vols. 8vo., full calf. London, 1809.
385 Historic Gallery of Portraits and Paintings. 3 vols.
     8vo., half Morocco. London.
386 Address to a Young Lady. 8vo., full calf. London,
     1796.
387 Price, U. An Essay on the Picturesque. 8vo., fine
     calf. London, 1794.
388 Blakey, Robt. Philosophy of Mind. 4 vols. 8vo.,
     full calf. London, 1848.
389 Noorthorick, Jno. Classical Dictionary. 2 vols. 8vo.,
     full calf. London, 1776.
390 Beatson, Robert. Political Index to the Histories of
     Great Britain and Ireland. 3 vols. 8vo., half calf.
     London, 1806.
391 Bowles, Wm. Lisle. Poetical Works of. 2 vols. 8vo.,
     full calf. New York, 1855.
392 Comyn, Sir Robert. History of the Western Empire.
     2 vols. 8vo., cloth. London, 1851.
393 Goethe. Memoirs of. 2 vols. 8vo., cloth. London,
     1824.
394 Kane, Elisha Kent. Arctic Explorations. 2 vols.
     8vo., full calf. Philadelphia, 1856.

395 Bryant, William Cullen. Letters of a Traveller. 8vo.,
     full Morocco. New York, 1851.
396 Dickens, Charles. Little Dorrit. 8vo., half Morocco.
     London, 1857.
397 Ainsworth, W. Harrison Rookwood. 8vo., half calf.
     Paris, 1836.
398 Junius. The Letters of. 2 vols. in 1. 8vo., full calf.
     New York, 1821.
399 Lempriere, J. Classical Dictionary. 8vo., half calf.
     London, 1844.
400 Bigelow, Jacob. Elements of Technology. 8vo., half
     Morocco. Boston, 1831.
401 Irving, Washington. Life of George Washington.
     5 vols. 8vo., half calf. New York, 1859.
402 Bury, Baroness Blaze de. Germania in 1850 Its
     Courts, Camps, and People. 8vo., cloth. London,
     1851.
403 Elements of Criticism. 2 vols. 8vo., full calf. Edin-
     burgh, 1774.
404 Burns, Robert. The Works of. 8vo., sheep. Phila-
     delphia, 1851.
405 Scott, Sir Walter. Poetical Works of. 8vo., sheep.
     Philadelphia, 1853.
406 Milton, Young, Gray, Beattie and Collins. Poetical
     Works of. 8vo., sheep. Philadelphia, 1849.
407 Sidney, Sir Philip. The Miscellaneous Works of.
     8vo., half Morocco. Boston, 1860.
408 Say, Thomas. American Entomology. Illustrated by
     Colored Figures from Original Drawings executed
     from Nature. 8vo., full roan. Philadelphia, 1828.
     In perfect condition.
409 Howitt, Wm. The Rural Life of England. 8vo., full
     calf. Philadelphia, 1841.
410 Everest, Rev. Chas. W. The Poets of Connecticut,
     with Biographical Sketches. 8vo., cloth. New
     York, 1847. Binding defective.
411 Southey, Robert. Select Works of. The British Poets,
     from Chaucer to Jonson, with Biographical Sketches.
     8vo., cloth. London, 1831.
412 Life of the Apostles ; also, Shephard's Island of St.
     Vincent. 2 vols. 8vo., full Morocco and cloth.

413   Francklin, Thomas. The Epistles of Phalaus. 8vo., sheep. London, 1749.

414   American Literary Magazine. Vol. 4. 8vo., full Morocco.

415   Moore, Thomas. The Poetical Works of. 8vo., full Morocco. New York, 1857.

416   Rush, Richard. A Residence at the Court of London. 2 vols. in 1. 8vo., cloth. London, 1845.

417   Colton, Calvin. Life, Correspondence and Speeches of Henry Clay. 6 vols. 8vo., half calf. New York, 1857.

418   Baines, Edward. History of the French Revolution. 2 vols. 8vo., cloth. New York, 1852.

419   Lamb, Charles. The Works of. 8vo., full calf. Philadelphia, 1857.

420   Scotia's Bards. 8vo., full calf. New York, 1854.

421   Chronicles of Eri. Being the History of the Goal Sciot Iber, or the Irish People. 2 vols. 8vo., half calf. London, 1822.

422   The Court and Times of James the First. Illustrated by authentic and confidential letters. 2 vols. 8vo., cloth. London, 1849.

423   Donovan, E. The Naturalists' Repository of Exotic Natural History, with 72 Elegantly Colored Plates. 2 vols. 8vo., full calf. London.

424   Westwood, J. O. Arcana Entomologica, or Illustrations of New and Rare and Interesting Insects. 2 vols. 8vo., full calf. London, 1845.

425   Milton, John. The Poetical Works of. 2 vols. 8vo., cloth. Lowell, 1848.

426   Hedge, Frederic H. Prose Writers of Germany. 8vo., full Morocco. Philadelphia, 1849.

427   Browner, James. History of the Highlands and of the Highland Clans, with an extensive selection from the hitherto Inedited Stuart Papers. 4 vols. 8vo., half calf. London, 1858.

428   Clarke, Mrs. Cowden. The Complete Concordance to Shakespeare. 8vo., half Morocco. Boston.

429   D'Aubigné, J. H. Merle. History of the Reformation. 8vo., half calf. Philadelphia, 1868

430 Ireland, Samuel. Graphic Illustrations of Hogarth, from Pictures, Drawings and Scarce Prints in the Possession of. 8vo., half calf. London, 1794. Water stained.
431 Rupp, I. Daniel. An Original History of the Religious Denominations Existing in the United States. 8vo., sheep. Philadelphia, 1844.
432 Bowen, Eli. Pictorial Sketch Book of Pennsylvania. 8vo., cloth. Philadelphia, 1853
433 Chatianbriand, Viscount de. The Genius of Christianity. 8vo., full Morocco. Baltimore, 1856. Water stained.
434 Marshall, James V. United States Manual of Biography and History. 8vo., cloth. Philadelphia, 1856.
435 Leaflets of Memory. 8vo., full Morocco. New York.
436 Duganne, A. The Poetical Works of. 8vo., full Morocco. Philadelphia, 1855.
437 Hawks, F. L. Narrative of Perry's Expedition to the China Seas and Japan. 8vo., full Morocco. New York, 1856.
438 Thiers, M. A. The Consulate and the Empire and the French Revolution. 2 vols. 8vo., half calf. London, 1850.
439 Portrait Gallery of Scotland, with Biographical Sketches. 8vo., cloth. Glasgow, 1838.
440 The Spectator, with Portraits. 8vo., half calf. London, 1857.
441 Loudon, L. E. Complete Works of. 8vo., full Morocco. Boston, 1856.
442 Brownell, Henry H. The Eastern or Old World. Illustrated. 4 vols. 8vo., cloth. New York, 1859.
443 Scott, Sir Walter. Poems by. 8vo., cloth. London.
444 Bethune, George W. Lays of Love and Faith. 8vo., cloth. Philadelphia.
445 Montgomery, James. Poetical Works of. 8vo., half calf. Boston, 1854.
446 Michaud, J. F. Histoire des Croisades. 6 vols. 8vo., half roan. Paris, 1841.
447 Rural Hours. Illustrated. 8vo., full Morocco. New York, 1851.
448 Lynch, W. F. The River Jordan and the Dead Sea. 8vo., sheep. Philadelphia, 1852.

449 Allison, A. History of Europe. 4 vols. 8vo., half
     calf. New York, 1855.
450 Prescott, W. H. The Conquest of Mexico. 3 vols.
     8vo., full Morocco. Boston, 1855.
451 Another copy. 3 vols. 8vo., full calf. Boston, 1855.
452 Prescott, W. H. The Conquest of Peru. 2 vols. 8vo.,
     full calf. Boston, 1855.
453 Prescott, W. H. Biographical and Critical Miscel-
     lanies. 8vo., full calf. Boston, 1855.
454 Prescott, W. H. History of the Reign of Philip the
     Second. 3 vols. 8vo., full calf. Boston, 1855.
455 Prescott, W. H. History of the Reign of Ferdinand
     and Isabella. 3 vols. 8vo., full calf. Boston, 1856.
456 Robertson, William. History of the reign of Charles
     the Fifth. 3 vols. 8vo., full calf. Boston, 1857.
457 Dickens, Chas. The Works of. Vols. 1, 2, 4 and 5,
     only. 4 vols. 8vo., half calf. Philadelphia.
458 Dickens, Chas. Household Words. 17 vols. 8vo.,
     half Morocco. London, 1850–1858.
459 National Cyclopœdia. 12 vols. in 6. 8vo., half calf.
     Boston, 1853.
460 Goldsmith, Oliver. History of the Earth and Animated
     Nature. Colored Illustrations. 2 vols. 8vo., half
     calf. Edinburgh.
461 Craik & Macfarlane. Pictorial History of England.
     4 vols. 8vo., half Morocco. New York, 1846.
462 Williams, Col. The Life and Times of the Late Duke
     of Wellington. Illustrated. 3 vols. London.
463 Mackenzie, Roderick. A Sketch of the War with
     Tippoo Sultaun. Vol. 1 only. 8vo., sheep. Cal-
     cutta, 1793.
464 Buckingham, J. S. Travels in Mesopotamia. 8vo.,
     half calf. London, 1827.
465 The Home Book of the Picturesque. 8vo., full Morocco.
     New York, 1852.
466 Buckler, J. C. Sixty Views of Endowed Grammar
     Schools, with Letter-press descriptions. 8vo., half
     Morocco. London, 1837. Plates water stained.
467 Constantinople and the Scenery of the Seven Churches
     of Asia Minor. Illustrated. 4to., full Morocco.
     London.

468 Dana, Charles A.   The United States.   Illustrated. 4to., full Morocco.   New York.
469 Jones' Views of the Seats, Mansions, Castles, etc., in England, Scotland and Wales.   8vo., cloth. London.
470 The Diadem for 1847.   Illustrated.   8vo., cloth. Philadelphia, 1847.
471 Knight's Vases and Ornaments.   8vo., cloth.   London.
472 Bartlett, W. H.   Finden's Views of the Ports, Harbors and Watering Places of Great Britian.   8vo., half Morocco.   London.
473 Bartlett, W. H.   Scenery and Antiquities of Ireland. 8vo., half calf.   London.
474 Bartlett.   Allom, etc., Syria, The Holy Lord, Asia Minor, etc.   Vols. 2 and 3 only.   2 vols.   8vo., half roan.   London.
475 Tyrrel, H.   History of the War with Russia.   Illustrated.   3 vols.   8vo., half Morocco.   London.
476 Pardoe, Miss.   The Beauties of the Bosphorus.   Illustrated by Bartlett.   8vo., full roan.   London, 1838.
477 Collas, Archilli.   The Authors of England.   A Series of Medallion Portraits of Modern Literary Characters, with Illustrative Notes.   8vo., cloth.   London, 1838.
478 Chronological Antiquities.   Vol. 3 only.   8vo., full calf.   London, 1752.
479 Wood, M.   Origin, Progress and Results of the late Decisive War in Mysore.   8vo., full calf.   London, 1810.
480 Kitto, John.   Gallery of Scripture Engravings.   4to., cloth.   Philadelphia, 1855.
481 The National Gallery of Pictures by Great Masters. 4to., cloth.   London.
482 Butterworth, John.   Concordance to the Holy Scripture.   4to., sheep,   Philadelphia, 1811.
483 Townson, R.   Travels in Hungary.   Illustrated.   4to., half calf.   London, 1787.
484 Lyall, Robert.   The Character of the Russians, with a Detailed History of Moscow.   Illustrated.   4to., half calf.   London, 1823.
485 Morgan, Lady.   2 vols. in 1.   4to., half calf.   London, 1821.

486 Garnett, T. Observations on a Tour through the
     Highlands and Part of the Western Isles of Scotland.
     Illustrated. 2 vols. in 1. 4to., calf. London, 1800.
487 Alexander, Wm. The History of Women. 2 vols in
     1. 4to., sheep. London, 1779. Binding defective.
488 Beattie, Wm. The Waldenses, or Protestant Valleys
     of Piedmont, Dauphiny and the Ban De La Roche.
     Illustrated by Bartlett and Brockendon. 4to.,
     cloth. London, 1838.
489 Leland, Thomas. The History of the Life and Reign
     of Philip, King of Macedon. 2 vols. 4to., full calf.
     London, 1758.
490 Modern London : being the History and Present State
     of the British Metropolis. Illustrated. 4to., half
     calf. London, 1804.
491 Prout & Harding. Views of Cities and Scenery in
     Italy, France and Switzerland, with Descriptions of
     the Plates by Thomas Roscoe. 2 vols. 8vo., cloth.
     London.
492 Allom, Thomas. France Illustrated : Exhibiting its
     Landscape Scenery, Antiquities, Military and
     Ecclesiastical Architecture. 4 vols. 8vo., half calf.
     London.
493 Carne, John. Syria, The Holy Land, Asia Minor, etc.
     Illustrated in a Series of Views drawn from Nature
     by W. H. Bartlett, William Purser and others. 2
     vols. 8vo., cloth. London.
494 Hinton, John H. The History and Topography of the
     United States of America. 2 vols. 4to., sheep.
     Boston.
495 Perouse, J. F. G., de la. A Voyage Round the World.
     2 vols. 4to., calf. London, 1799.
496 The Artist's Portfolio. 2 vols. 4to., cloth. London.
497 The Andalusian Annual for 1837. Colored Illustra-
     tions. 4to., cloth. London, 1836.
498 Poems of the Death of Lord Nelson. In Latin and
     English. Written for the Turtonian Medals. 4to.,
     full calf. London, 1807.
499 Engravings from Paintings by Modern Masters. 2 vols.
     4to., cloth.
500 Collas, Achille. The Authors of England, with Illus-
     trative Notices by Henry F. Chorley. 2 vols. 8vo.,
     cloth. London, 1838.

501 Alexander, W. The Costumes of China. 4to., half calf. London.
502 Musical Library. 4to., cloth. London.
503 A Complete History of Theatrical Entertainments, Dramas, Masques, and Triumphs at the English Court, with Engravings by Findin. Small folio, cloth. London.
504 Chalon, A. E. Portraits of the Children of the Nobility 4to., cloth. London, 1841.
505 Rehbug, Frederick. Lady Hamilton's Attitudes. 4to., cloth. 1794.
506 Royal Gallery of Pictures. 4to., boards.
507 Views in the Vicinity of Bristol and Chepstow. Long 8vo., cloth.
508 Pinelli, B. Twenty-seven Etchings, Illustrative of Italian Manners and Costumes. Folio. cloth. Rome, 1844.
509 Findin, Edward. The Beauties of Moore. Folio, cloth. London.
510 Birdford, Denicon. The Wonders of the Heavens. 4to., half Morocco. Boston, 1837.
511 Sauvan, M. Picturesque Tour of the Seine. Illustrated, with highly-finished and colored Engravings, from Drawings by Pugen and Gendall. 4to., cloth. London, 1821.
512 Lear, Edward. Illustrated Excursions in Italy. Folio, cloth. London, 1846.
513 The Costume of Turkey. Illustrated by a Series of Engravings with Descriptions in English and French. Folio, roan. London, 1802
514 Amsinck, Paul. Trowbridge Wells. Illustrated by Letitia Byrne. 4to., half Morocco. London.
515 Bradford, Rev. Wm. Sketches of the Country, Character and Costume in Portugal and Spain. Illustrated. Folio, half roan. London.
516 Heath's Portfolio of Engravings. Folio, half Morocco. London.
517 Uwins, Thos. The Costumes of the University of Oxford. Illustrated by a series of Engravings. 4to., boards. London, 1815.

518 Select Views in Italy with Topographical and Historical Descriptions in English and French.   2 vols.
Long 4to., cloth. London, 1792

519 Scenes from the Life of Moses; a Series of Twenty
Engravings in outline. Designed by H. C. Selous,
and engraved by Charles Rolls. Folio, paper.
London, 1850.

520 Grindlay, Capt. Robert Melville. Scenery, Costumes
and Architecture, chiefly on the Western Side of
India. Folio, half Morocco. London, 1826.

521 Burnett, Bishop. History of his own Time. 2 vols.
Folio, half roan.

522 Nicolas, Sir N. H.   History of the Orders of Knight-
hood of the British Empire; of the Order of the
Guelphs of Hanover; and of the Medals, Clasps
and Crosses conferred for Naval and Military Ser-
vices. 4 vols. Folio, cloth. London, 1842.

523 Penn, William. Select Works of; to which is prefixed
a Journal of his Life. Folio, full calf. London,
1771.

524 Turnbull, George. A Treatise on Ancient Painting.
Illustrated with Fifty Pieces of Ancient Paintings.
Folio, calf. London, 1740.

525 Allason, Thomas. Picturesque Views of the Antiquities of Polo in Istria. Folio, half roan. London,
1819.

526 Bury, Lady Charlotte. The Three Great Sanctuaries
of Tuscany, Valambrosa, Camaldoli and Laverna.
Illustrated. Long 4to., half roan. London, 1833.

527 Pontoppidau, Rev. Erich. The Natural History of
Norway. Small folio, calf. London, 1755.

528 Finden, W. & E. Tableau of National Character, Beauty
and Costumes, in a Series of Illustrations. 2 vols.
in 1. Folio, half calf. London.

529 Nattes, J. C. The Beauties of Scotland. Long 4to.,
cloth. 1848.

530 Church, John. A Cabinet of Quadrupeds, consisting
of Highly-Finished Engravings, by James Tookey,
from Drawings by Julius Ibbetson. 2 vols. 4to.,
full calf. London, 1805.

531 Gleanings of Natural History, being a Series of Plates.
4to., full Morocco.

532 Brown, Richard. The Rudiments of Drawing Cabinet
     and Upholstery Furniture. 4to., boards. London,
     1835.
533 Drury, D   Illustrations of Natural History, wherein
     are exhibited upwards of Two Hundred and Twenty
     Figures of Exotic Insects. Vols. 2 and 3 only. 2
     vols. 4to. sheep. London, 1773.
534 Cave, William. Antiquitates Apostolicæ. Small folio,
     half sheep. London, 1676.
535 Bell's Pantheon. 2 vols. in 1. 4to., full calf. London,
     1790 Binding defective.
536 Malte-Brun, M. Universal Geography. 3 vols. 4to.,
     sheep. Boston, 1834.
537 Burnett, Bishop. The Sacred Theory of the Earth.
     4to., sheep. London, 1816.
538 Dana, Chas. A. The United States. Illustrated. 4to.,
     full Morocco. New York.
539 Wraxall, N. W. History of France. Vol. 1 only. 4to.,
     full calf. London, 1795.
540 Froissart, Sir John. Chronicles of England, France
     and Spain. 8vo., half roan. New York.
541 Park, Mungo. Travels in the Interior Districts of
     Africa. 8vo., half roan. London, 1816.
542 Payne's Pictorial World. 3 vols. 8vo., half calf.
     London.
543 Wilkes, Chas. The United States Exploring Expedition.
     6 vols. 4to., half Morocco. Philadelphia, 1846.
544 Burney, James. Chronological History of the Dis-
     coveries in the South Sea. 5 vols. 4to., half calf.
     London, 1803.
545 Fancy Ornaments. 8vo., boards.
546 Hach, Charles. The New Gallery of British Engrav-
     ings. 8vo., cloth. London, 1846.
547 Beattie, William. Scotland Illustrated. Vol. 2 only.
     8vo., calf. London, 1838.
548 Darwin, Erasmus. Zoonomia, or the Laws of Organic
     Life. 2 vols. 8vo., half Morocco. London, 1796.
549 Transactions of the American Philosophical Society.
     Vols. 1 to 6. Morocco bound, and vol. 7, unbound.
     7 vols. 8vo., cloth.

550   Turner, J. M. W.   Liber Fluviorum, or River Scenery
       of France, depicted in 61 Line Engravings, with
       Descriptive Letterpress by Leitch Ritchie. 8vo.,
       cloth. London, 1857.
551   Cunningham, Allen. The Cabinet Gallery of Pictures.
       Vol. 1 only. 8vo., half Morocco. London, 1833.
552   Wright, Thomas. History of Scotland. Illustrated
       with Portraits of Eminent Scotchmen and Celebrated
       Personages connected with Scottish History. 3
       vols. 8vo., half Morocco. London.
553   Batty, Cockburn and Light. German, French, Italian,
       Swiss and Sicilian Scenery. 5 vols. 8vo., half
       Morocco. London.
554   Longacre & Herring. National Portrait Gallery of
       Distinguished Americans. 3 vols. 8vo., half
       Morocco. Philadelphia, 1835.
555   Fartlett, W. H. History of the United States, continued
       by B. B. Woodward. 3 vols. 8vo., half Morocco.
       New York.
556   Canova, Antonio.   The Works of, in Sculpture and
       Modelling. Engraved in Outline by Henry Moses.
       3 vols. 8vo., half roan. London, 1849.
557   Whyte, Samuel. The Shamrock ; or, Hibernian Cresses.
       8vo., half Morocco. Dublin, 1772.
558   House of Peeresses. 8vo., half Morocco. No title
       page.
559   Irving, Washington. Washington's Earlier Years.
       8vo., full Morocco. New York, 1857.
560   Middiman's Select Views in Great Britian. Long 8vo.,
       half roan. London.
561   Watts, W. The Seats of the Nobilty and Gentry.
       Long 8vo., half Roan. London.
562   Sandby, P. Select Views in England, Scotland and
       Ireland. Long 8vo., boards. London, 1778.
563   Our Globe Illustrated. Long 8vo., half roan. Phila-
       delphia.
564   Bryan, Michael. A Biographical and Critical Diction-
       ary of Painters and Engravers, with the Ciphers,
       Monograms and Marks used by each Engraver.
       8vo., half Morocco. London, 1858.
565   Kinsey, Rev. William. Portugal. Illustrated. 8vo.,
       half Morocco. London, 1829.

566 Sanderson's Biography of the Signers to the Declaration of Independence. 8vo., half Morocco. Philadelphia, 1848.

567 Campbell, Thomas. Specimens of the British Poets. 8vo., full Morocco. Philadelphia, 1853.

568 Mossinger, Philip. The Plays of. 8vo., cloth. New York, 1857.

569 Illustrations—Landscape, Historical and Antiquarian— to the Poetical Works of Sir Walter Scott. 8vo., half Morocco, London.

570 Carlyle, Thomas. Critical and Miscellaneous Essays. 8vo., cloth. Philadelphia, 1850.

571 Wraxall, Sir N. W. Historical Memoirs. 8vo., cloth. Philadelphia, 1845.

572 McCulloch's Universal Gazetteer. 2 vols. 8vo., sheep. New York, 1847.

573 Darell, Rev. Wm. History of Dover Castle. 8vo., half sheep. London, 1786.

574 Chamber's Edinburgh Journal. Vols. 12 to 20 inclusive. 9 vols. 8vo., cloth.

575 Die Kleinen Leiden des Menschlicken Librus. Illustrirt von J. J. Grandville. 8vo., half Morocco. Leipzig, 1846.

576 Heber, Rev. R. Narrative of a Journey through the Upper Provinces of India, 1824 and 1825. 2 vols. 8vo., boards. Philadelphia, 1828.

577 Brayley, Edward W. London and Middlesex. 5 vols. 8vo., half calf. London, 1810.

578 Gil Blas. Vol. 2 only. 8vo., calf. Binding defective. New York, 1824.

579 Fairfield's Works. 8vo., cloth.

580 Irving, W. Oliver Ooldsmith. 8vo., cloth. New York, 1849.

581 Stewart's Philosophy; also, Greek and English Lexicon. 2 vols. 8vo., cloth.

582 Wirt, William. Sketches of the Life and Character of Patrick Henry. 8vo., sheep. Hartford, 1854.

583 9 Books, assorted.

584 Trusler, Rev. John. The Habitable World Described, or the Present State of the People in all Parts of the Globe, from North to South. 20 vols. 8vo., calf. London, 1788–1797. Binding in bad condition.

BOTANICAL WORKS.

585 Systema Algarum. 16mo., calf. Lundæ, 1824.

586 Rafinesque, C. S. Medical Flora. 2 vols. in 1. 16mo.,
Morocco. Philadelphia, 1828.

587 Noll, H. R. Flora of Pennsylvania. 12mo., roan.
Philadelphia, 1851.

588 Nuttall, Thos. The Genera of North American Plants.
12mo., sheep. Philadelphia, 1818.

589 Barton, W. P. C. Compendium Floræ Philadelphicæ.
2 vols. 12mo., sheep. Philadelphia, 1818.

590 Coultas, H. The Principles of Botany. 12mo., cloth.
Philadelphia, 1855.

591 Parkinson, Jos. Fossil Organic Remains. 12mo.,
sheep. London, 1830.

592 Coultas, H. The Plants. 12mo., cloth. Philadelphia,
1855.

593 Nuttall, T. Introduction to Botany. 12mo., boards.
Cambridge, 1830.

594 Darlington, Wm. Flora Cestrica. 12mo., half calf.
West Chester, 1837.

595 Bunardin, J. K. Botanical Harmony Delineated.
12mo., sheep. Worcester, 1797.

596 Linnæi, Caroli. Species Plantarum. 2 vols. 12mo.,
old calf. Holmiæ, 1753.

597 Miscellanies. 12mo., half calf.

598 Hales, Stephen. Statical Essays. 2 vols. 12mo.,
full calf. London 1769.

599 Aiton, William. Hortus Kewensis. 5 vols. 8vo.,
sheep. London, 1810.

600 Loddiges's Botanical Cabinet. 7 vols. Small 4to.,
half calf. London, 1817.

601 Linnæi Caroli Systema Vegetabilium. 3 vols. 8vo.,
sheep. Gottingæ, 1825.

602 Bryologia Universa. 8vo., sheep. Lipsiæ, 1823.

603 Thunberg, Carol Pet. Flora Capensis. 8vo., sheep
Stuttgardtiæ, 1823.

604 Prush, Frederick. Flora Americæ Septentrionalis.
8vo., sheep. London, 1816.

605 Gray, Asa. Botany of the Northern United States. 12mo., cloth. Boston, 1848.

606 Steudel & Hochstetter. Enumeratio Plantarum. 12mo., boards. Stuttgardtiæ, 1826.

607 De Candolle, Aug. Prodromus Systematis, Naturalis Regni, Vegetabilus. 13 vols. 8vo., sheep. Parisiis, 1824.

608 Steudel, Ernesto. Nomenclator Botanicus. 2 vols. 8vo., half sheep. Stuttgardtiæ, 1821.

609 Smith, James Edward. The English Flora. 4 vols. 8vo., cloth. London.

610 Hooker, Sir W. J. Niger Flora. 8vo., cloth. London, 1849.

611 Lindley, John. Introduction to Botany. 8vo., cloth. London, 1839.

612 Lindley, John. Flora Medica. 8vo., cloth. London, 1838.

613 Lindley, John. The Vegetable Kingdom. 8vo., cloth, London, 1853.

614 Broomfield, W. A. Flora Vectensis. 8vo., cloth. London, 1866.

615 Hooker, W. J. Musci Exotici. 2 vols. 8vo., cloth. London, 1818.

616 Loudon, J. C. Encyclopædia of Gardening. 8vo., cloth. London, 1850.

617 De Candolle, Aug. Vegetable Organography. 2 vols. 8vo., cloth. London, 1841.

618 Richard, A. Elements of Botany and Vegetable Physiology. 8vo., cloth. Edinburgh, 1831.

619 Muhlenberg, D. H. Descriptio Uberior Graminum. 8vo., sheep. Philadelphia, 1817.

620 Smith, James Edward. Introduction to Physiological and Systematical Botany. 8vo., sheep. Philadelphia, 1814.

621 Lindley, John. Natural System of Botany. 8vo., half sheep. New York, 1831.

622 Good, John Mason. Book of Nature. 8vo., sheep. Hartford, 1837.

623 Barton, B. S. Elements of Botany. 8vo., half sheep. Philadelphia, 1803.

624 Sullivant, W. S. The Musci and Hepaticæ of the United States. 8vo., cloth. New York, 1856.

625   Sweet, Robert.   Geraniaceæ.   The National Order of
         Geranea.   Illustrated by Colored Figures and De-
         scriptions.   5 vols.   8vo., half Morocco,   London.
         1820–1822.
626   Hooker, W. J.   Exotic Flora.   3 vols.   8vo.,   half
         Morocco.   Edenburgh, 1823.
627   Muhlenberg, Henry.   Catologus Plantaium Americæ
         Septutrionalis.   8vo., half roan.   Lancaster, Pa.,
         1813.
628   Schweinitz, Rev. L. D. De.   Monograph of the North
         American Species of the Genus Carex.   8vo., half
         sheep.   New York, 1825.
629   Coultas, H.   What may be Learned from the Tree.
         8vo., cloth.   Philadelphia, 1860.
630   Thornton's Elements of Botany.   8vo., boards.
631   Wood, Alphonse.   Class Book of Botany.   12mo.,
         cloth.   New York, 1861.
631½   Robin and Rofinesque.   Flora of Louisiana.   12mo.,
         paper.   New York, 1817.
632   Smith, J. E.   Grammar of Botany.   12mo., paper.   New
         York, 1822.
633   Linnæi, Caroli.   Systema Vegetabilium.   12mo., half
         sheep.   Gottingæ, 1827.
634   Linnæi, Caroli.   Philosophia Botanica.   12mo., sheep.
         Vindobomæ, 1770.
635   Piton, Joseph.   Institutions Rei Herbariæ.   8vo.,   No
         binding.   Parisiis, 1719.
636   Another copy.   8vo., old calf.   Parisiis, 1700.
637   Baubinus.   Theatre Botanica.   8vo., vellum.   1676.
         Title page destroyed.
638   Acharius Erik.   Lichenographia Universalis.   4to.,
         half sheep.   Gottingæ, 1810.
639   Hedwig, Joannis.   Species Muscorum Frondosorum.
         4to., half sheep.   Lipsiæ, 1801.
640   Bauhini, Cospair.   Theatri Botanici.   4to., old calf.
         Basiliæ, 1671.
641   Haller, Aucton von.   Bibliotheca Botanica.   2 vols.
         4to., full calf.   Tiguri, 1771.
642   Darwin, Erasmus.   Phytologia.   4to., half Morocco.
         London, 1800.
643   Botanic Garden.   2 vols. in 1.   4to., half Morocco.
         London, 1791.

644 Bertolonii, Antonii. Arnoenitates Italicæ. 4to., paper. Bononiæ, 1819.

645 Buxbaum, J. C. Plantarum Minus Cognitarum Centuria. 4to., full calf. Petropoli, 1733.

646 Barton, W. P. C. Vegetable Materia Medica. 4to. Boston and Philadelphia, 1817.

647 Grew, Nehemjah. The Anatomy of Plants. Small folio, old calf. 1682.

648 Matthioli, Petri Andreæ. In Libros Sex Pedacii Dioscoridis Anazarbei de Medica Materia. Small folio, vellum. Venetiis, 1558.

649 Verzascham, Du Bernhardum. Herbarium Virorum Eperientissimorum. Small folio, vellum. No title page.

650 Chabræo, Dominico. Stirpium Icones et Seiagraphia cum Omnibus Iuæ de Plantarum. Small folio, vellum. Genevæ, 1677.

651 The British Fuci. Selected Plates, with Letterpress Descriptions in English and Latin. 4to., boards.

652 Curtis, William. Flora Londinensis, or Plates and Descriptions of such Plants as grow wild in the Environs of London. 3 vols. Folio, half roan, London, 1777.

653 Gray, Asa. Botany, Phanerogamia (United States Exploring Expidition, 1837–1842) with Atlas containing 100 plates. 2 vols. Text 4to., half Morocco, and Atlas folio, half Morocco. 2 vols. New York, 1854 and 1857.

654 Sweet, Robert. The British Flower Garden, with upwards of 700 Colored Plates from Drawings by E. D. Smith. Vol. 6 wanting, 6 vols. only. 8vo., cloth. London, 1838.

655 Lindley, John. Edwards' Botanical Register, with Colored Illustrations. 10 vols. 8vo., cloth. London, 1838.

756 Botanical Magazine, with Index. 44 vols. in 23 vols, 8vo., half calf. London, 1787–1816.

———

657 Conversations. Lexikon du Gegenwart. 5 vols. 8vo., half sheep. Leipzig, 1838.

658 Conversations. Lexikon. 12 vols. 8vo., half sheep
    Leipzig, 1833
659 Hartman, Franz. Therapie a Kuter Kraukheitsforman.
    2 vols. 12mo., half calf. Leipzig, 1834.
660 Linne, Sir Chas. System of Nature. 7 vols. 8vo.,
    half calf. London, 1806.
661. Niles' Register, Sept., 1811, to July, 1849. 75 vols.
    8vo. and 4to., half calf. Philadelphia.
662 The History of Rinaldo Rinaldini. 3 vols. in 1. 18mo.,
    roan. New York, 1854.
663 Lee, George. Mantle of Elijah; also, Margaret. 2
    vols. 12mo., cloth.
664 Life and Letters of Elizabeth, Duchess of Gordon; also,
    Paul of Tarsus. 2 vols. 12mo., cloth.
665 Sigourney, Mrs. Letters to Mothers; also, Woman.
    2 vols. 12mo., cloth.
666 Hedge, F. H. The Primeval World. 12mo., cloth.
    Boston, 1870.
667. Gilfillan, Geo. Modern Literature. 12mo., cloth.
    New York, 1846.
668 Graham, Rev. John. Siege of Londonderry. 12mo.,
    cloth. Philadelphia, 1844.
669 Alcott, A. Bronson. Record of a School, Our Life in
    China, and a Rambling Story. 3 vols, 12mo.,
    cloth.
670 Schefer, Leopold. The Married Life of Albert Durer.
    12mo., boards. Boston, 1849.
671 Boone, Rev. T. Charles. The Marriage Looking Glass.
    12mo., cloth. London, 1848.
672 Alger, W. R. The Friendships of Women. 12mo.,
    cloth. Boston, 1868.
673 Alcot, A. Bronson. Concord Days; also, Domestic
    Life. 2 vols. 12mo., cloth.
674 Matthews, C. Chanticleer. Illustrated by Dailey.
    12mo., boards. New York.
675 Murray, John Fisher. Father Tom and the Pope.
    12mo., cloth. Philadelphia.
676 Hale, Mrs. Poems by. 3 copies. 12mo., boards.
677 Arnold, Geo. Poems by. Pierpont's Poetical Works,
    Poems by Caldwell and Poems by Cist. 4 vols.
    12mo., cloth.

678 Hamilton, Gail.   Stumbling Blocks, Skirmishes and
     Sketches, A New Atmosphere, and Woman's
     Wrongs. 4 vols. 12mo., cloth. Boston.
679 Follen, E. L.   Home Dramas; also, Drawing-room
     Plays. 2 vols. 12mo., cloth.
680 Bryant, William Cullen.   The Life, Character and
     Genius of Washington Irving. 12mo., cloth. New
     York, 1860.
681 Peterson, Henry.   Faire-mount. 12mo., cloth. Phila-
     delphia, 1874.
682 Wells, Anna Maria.   Poems by.   12mo., cloth.
     Boston, 1830.
683 Flagg, W. J.   European Vineyards, The Skeleton
     Monk, and 500 Employments Adapted to Women.
     3 vols. 12mo., cloth.
684 Sermons on Abraham Lincoln.   2 vols., assorted.
     12mo., cloth.
685 Leslie's, Miss.   Cook Book. 2 vols., assorted. 2 vols.
     12mo., cloth.
686 Urbino, Day, and others.   Art Recreation.   12mo.,
     cloth. Boston, 1864.
687 Talmage, T. De Witt.   Sermons by. 2 vols.   12mo.,
     cloth. New York, 1872–3.
688 Bremer, Fredrika.   The Home and The Neighbors.
     2 vols. 12mo., cloth.
689 Prenticeana; or, Wit and Humor in Paragraphs. 12mo.,
     cloth. New York, 1860.
690 Peterson, Chas. J.   The Old Stone Mansion, David,
     the King of Israel, and the Roman Exile.   3 vols.
     12mo., cloth.
691 Houdin, Robert.   Memoirs of; also, Memories by.
     2 vols. 12mo., cloth.
692 Wilson, R. A.   Mexico and its Religion.   12mo.,
     cloth. New York, 1855.
693 Arnat, Rev. William.   Autobiography of.   12mo.,
     cloth. New York, 1878.
694 Gregorovius, F. Corsica. 12mo., cloth. Philadelphia,
     1855.
695 Clapp, Rev. T.   Autobiographical Sketches; Essays
     in Biography. 2 vols. And Thoughts on Preach-
     ing. 4 vols. 12mo., cloth.

696   Brainerd, Rev. T. Life of; Life of John Foster. 2
       vols. 12mo., cloth.
697   Macleod, Norman. Parish Papers. 12mo., cloth. New
       York, 1863.
698   Hanna, William. The Wars of the Huguenots. 12mo.,
       cloth. New York, 1872.
699   Sedgwick, C. M. Life and Letters of. New York,
       1871.
700   Abbott, J. S. C. Confidential Correspondence of the
       Emperor Napoleon and the Empress Josephine.
       12mo., cloth. New York, 1856.
701   Boise, J. R. First Three Books of Xenophon's. Ana-
       basis, Plutarch and Plautus. 3 vols. 12mo., half
       roan and cloth.
702   Miller, Joaquin. Songs of the Sierras. 12mo., cloth,
       Boston, 1871.
703   Walter Ogelby; also, The Opium Habit. 2 vols.
       12mo., cloth.
704   The Gayworthys. 12mo., cloth. Boston.
705   Robertson, Flo. Sermon by; also, Studies in the
       Field and Forest. 2 vols. 12mo., cloth.
706   Degerando, Baron. Self-Education; also, The Lan-
       guages without a Master. 2 vols. 12mo., cloth.
707   Home Pastimes. 12mo., cloth. Boston, 1867.
708   Hale, Mrs. Liberia. 4 copies. 12mo., cloth.
709   Vericom's Modern French Literature; also, The
       Prophet of Fire. 2 vols. 12mo., cloth.
710   Day, Henry. A Lawyer Abroad. 12mo., cloth. New
       York, 1874.
711   Guthrie, Thomas. Autobiography of. 2 vols. 12mo.,
       cloth. New York, 1874.
712   Loomis, Elias. The Progress of Astronomy. 12mo.,
       New York, 1850.
713   French, B. B., FritzClarence. 12mo., half roan,
       Washington, 1844.
714   Channing, Walter. A Physician's Vacation. 18mo.,
       cloth. Boston, 1856.
715   The Second Presbyterian Church, 1743-1876. 12mo.,
       cloth.
716   Cockburn, Lord. Life of Lord Jeffrey. 12mo., cloth,
       Philadelphia, 1856.

717 Duniway, A. S.   David and Anna Matson.   12mo.,
      cloth.   New York, 1876.
718 Alger, W. R.   History of the Doctrine of a Future
      Life.   8vo., cloth.   Philadelphia, 1864.
719 Amelia.   Poems by.   2 copies.   8vo., Morocco and
      cloth.
720 Wheeler, Edward.   Croydon Centennial.   1866.   8vo.,
      cloth.
721 Hilliard, Henry W.   Speeches and Addresses.   8vo.,
      cloth.   New York, 1855.
722 Letters of Commodore Stockton to the New York
      Evening Post.   8vo., cloth.   Philadelphia, 1864.
723 Bouvier, Hannah M.   Familiar Astronomy.   8vo.,
      Philadelphia, 1857.
724 Beecher, Henry Ward.   Morning Exercises.   8vo.,
      cloth.   New York, 1871.
725 Tyerman, Rev. L.   The Life and Times of the Rev.
      John Wesley.   Vols: 1 and 3 only.   2 vols., 8vo.,
      cloth.   New York, 1872.
726 Beecher, H. W.   Sermons by.   2 vols.   8vo., cloth.
      New York, 1868
727 Street, A. B.   The Poems of; also, Chief of the Pil-
      grims.   2 vols.   8vo., cloth.
728 Lewis, E. A.   Records of the Heart; also, Philadelphia
      Lectures.   2 vols.   8vo., cloth.
729 Duganne, A.   The Poetical Works of.   8vo., cloth.
      Philadelphia, 1855.
730 Farmer's Every-day Book.   8vo., full Morocco.
      Auburn, N. Y., 1850.
731 Report of the Secretary of the Navy.   2 vols.   8vo.,
      half sheep.
732 Alexander, Dr. J. W.   Life of.   8vo., cloth.   New York,
      1854.
733 Paine, Dr. Martyn.   Physiology of the Soul and
      Instinct.   8vo., cloth.   New York, 1872.
734 Horner, C. R. B.   Medical Topography of Brazil and
      Uruguay.   8vo., cloth.   Philadelphia, 1845.
735 Bethlehem Seminary Souvenir.   8vo., cloth.   Philadel-
      phia, 1858.
736 Index to Harper's Magazine.   Vols. 1–40.   8vo., cloth.
737 Sacred Annual.   8vo., cloth.   Philadelphia, 1850.

738   Gil Blas. Illustrated by Smirke. 4 vols. in 2. 18mo.,
      cloth. London, 1822.
739   Sterne, Laurence. Tristam Shandy 12mo., cloth.
      New York, 1857.
740   The Arabian Nights. 8vo., cloth. Philadelphia, 1856.
741   L'Ardeche, M. Laurent. History of Napoleon, with
      Illustrations after Designs by Horace Vernet. 2
      vols. 8vo., half calf. London.
742   Prior, Matthew. Poems on Several Occasions. 2 vols.
      16mo., full calf. London, 1754.
743   Burke, Edmund. Reflections on the Revolution in
      France. 8vo., sheep. London, 1791.
744   Sparks, Jaud. The Writings of George Washington,
      Vol. 11 wanting. 11 vols. 8vo., half sheep. Boston,
      1837.
745   Hazard Ebenezer. Historical Collection, consisting of
      State Papers and other Documents intended as Ma-
      terials for a History of the United States. 2 vols.
      4to., half calf. Philadelphia, 1792.
746   South Kensington Museum Art Handbooks. 9 vols.
      12mo., cloth.
747   Ritzsch, Moritz. Illustrations to Goethe's Faust. Long
      12mo., cloth.
748   Richardson & Watts. Complete Practical Treatise on
      Acids, Alkalies and Salts. 3 vols. 8vo., cloth.
      London, 1867.
749   Foster, John Y New Jersey and the Rebellion. 8vo.,
      sheep. Newark, 1868,
750   Oswandel, J. Jacob. Notes of the Mexican War. 8vo.,
      cloth. Philadelphia, 1885.
751   Hamersly, L. R. Records of Living Officers of the
      U. S. Navy and Marine Corps. 8vo., cloth. Phila-
      delphia, 1870.
752   Mahan, D. H. An Elementary Course of Permanent
      Fortifications. 8vo., cloth. New York, 1874.
753   Warren, Jos. H. Hernia. 8vo., cloth. Boston, 1881.
754   Grant, James. Superstitions, Demonology, Witchcraft,
      and Popular Delusions. 8vo., cloth, and uncut
      copy. Leith.
755   Nevin, Alfred. Men of Mark of Cumberland Valley,
      Pa., 1776-1876. 8vo., half roan. Philadelphia,
      1876.

756 Werner, Carl, Nile Students. 6 parts. Folio, paper.
757 Viardot, Louis. The Masterpieces of French Art. 2
      vols. Folio, half Morocco. Philadelphia.
758 Masterpieces of French Art. 11 Plates in Portfolio.
759 Masterpieces of German Art. 2 vols. Folio, half
      Morocco. Philadelphia.
760 Findley Estate. Executive Documents. Vol. 2, Parts
      2, 4, 5, 6 and 7. 5 vols. 4to, sheep.
761 Explorations for a Railroad Route from the Mississippi
      River to the Pacific Ocean. Vols. 1, 8, 9, 10 and
      12. 6 vols. 4to., half calf and cloth.
762 Congressional Globe. Vols. 21 and 23. Senate Docu-
      ments. Vol. 13, Part 2. 3 vols. 4to., half calf and
      sheep.
763 Military Commission to Europe. 2 vols. 4to., cloth.
764 Cassin, John. Mammaology and Ornithology; "United
      States Exploring Expedition." 4to., cloth. Phila-
      delphia, 1858.
765 Scott's Commentary. Vols. 1, 3, 4 and 5. 4 vols. only.
      4to., sheep.
766 28 Reports, assorted.
767-774 8 bundles Books.
774½ Lot. Battles of the United States by Sea and by Land.
775 do The History of Ireland.
776 do Harpers' Weekly.
777 do Century Magazine.
778 Large lot Magazines.
779 9 Books, assorted.
780 8   do
781-787 7 bundles School Books, assorted.
788 8 Reports, assorted.
789-797 9 bundles Books, assorted.
798 Lot Books, assorted.
799 do Pamphlets, assorted.

M. THOMAS & SONS,

Auctioneers.

www.ingramcontent.com/pod-product-compliance
Lightning Source LLC
Chambersburg PA
CBHW022206020726
47496CB00008B/2903